Ninja Panda and Me

Contents

T0321625

Written by Catherine Baker

Illustrated by Jan Smith

Collins

Who and what is in this story?

Listen and say

Lucy

Tom

Ninja Panda

skateboard

Tom's mum

May

My best friend

My name's Tom. I'm seven years old and I like aliens, **ninjas**, chocolate and my best friend, Lucy.

Lucy often comes to my house to play. I live by a big park and Mum often takes us there. We like to play football and run around.

There's a fantastic tree in the park. It's great for us to climb up.

5

One day, we had a picnic in the tree! Mum put
sandwiches, orange juice and some little
cakes in a bag. I put the bag on my back and
climbed up the tree with Lucy.

We took all the food out of the bag and ate it
in the tree. It was a fantastic picnic.

Two days with Ninja Panda!

Lucy always brings her Ninja Panda with her. Ninja Panda is fantastic! He plays in all our games. He has a black ninja **mask** and a **cape**. He helps us to **fight** monsters in our games and he always **wins**.

One day, I said to Lucy, "Can I **borrow** Ninja Panda for a day or two?"

Lucy thought about it.

"OK," she said. "You can borrow Ninja Panda, but can I borrow your new skateboard, please?"

That Saturday, I went to Lucy's house.
I gave Lucy the skateboard, and she gave me
Ninja Panda.

"I want Ninja Panda back on Monday, please!"
said Lucy. "You can have your skateboard on
Monday, too."

I took Ninja Panda to my house. "Fantastic!"
I thought. "Now I can have *two days* with
Ninja Panda!"

First, Ninja Panda and I fought some monsters in the garden. Ninja Panda won (again!).
We looked for aliens, but we didn't find any.
Then I got my big boat and Ninja Panda crossed the sea in it (I mean the bath)!

At lunch, Ninja Panda sat next to my plate.
He watched me eat my fish and chips. But *he*
didn't eat any lunch!

After lunch, Ninja Panda and I went to the park. Mum came too, with my little sister, May.

Ninja Panda and I climbed the tree and sat at the top. We could see everything from there.

We saw Mum and May by the river. But then
we saw something terrible! May fell down and
hurt her leg. She started crying.

I climbed down the tree. I ran to May
and **hugged** her. Mum hugged her, too.

I found a sweet and gave it to May.
That helped her to stop crying!

We went home and Mum cleaned May's leg.
Then we ate dinner. After dinner,
May and I watched TV, then May went to bed.

Where is he?

I cleaned my teeth before I went to
bed, too. Then I thought about Ninja Panda.
Where was he? I went down the stairs
and looked on the sofa. No Ninja Panda.
He wasn't under the table or in the kitchen.

"Mum!" I shouted. "I can't find Ninja Panda!"
I sat down on the floor and started crying.

Mum helped me to look for Ninja Panda.
We looked and looked, but we couldn't
find him.

"Don't worry, Tom," said Mum. "Let's find Ninja Panda in the morning. Go to bed now."

But it was very difficult to go to sleep that night!

20

I thought about Ninja Panda. Where was he?
I thought about Lucy. She loved Ninja Panda!

"I can give her my skateboard," I thought.
But that made me sad.

My good idea

I thought about Ninja Panda all night.
At breakfast, I had a good idea. "The park!"
I shouted. "Mum, let's go to the park – now!"

We all went to the park. I ran to the big tree. I thought that Ninja Panda was under the tree. I ran around the tree and looked and looked, but there was no Ninja Panda.

Then Mum said, "Look up there, Tom!"

I looked up and there was Ninja Panda! He was in the tree! I climbed up quickly and helped him down.

Ninja Panda's mask was very dirty and there was a **hole** in his cape!

"Oh no!" I said. "Lucy can't see this!"

But then I had an idea. "Don't worry, Ninja Panda," I said. "You can have a beautiful new cape and mask!"

New clothes!

Ninja Panda and I ran home. I made a new cape and mask from an old red T-shirt.

Mum washed Ninja Panda and I put him in his new clothes. Ninja Panda looked very good!

That afternoon, Ninja Panda and I didn't go to the park. We played in the garden and I was very careful with him.

We looked for aliens, but we didn't find any. We fought some small monsters, and Ninja Panda won!

The next day was Monday. I took Ninja Panda to Lucy's house.

"I like Ninja Panda's new cape and mask!" said Lucy. "How did he get them?"

"It's a long story," I said.

"Tell me later," she said. She gave me my skateboard back, and said, "First, let's have a game of aliens on skateboards."

So Lucy, Ninja Panda and I played aliens on skateboards all day.

Mini-dictionary

Listen and read

borrow (verb) If you **borrow** something, you use something that belongs to someone else for a short time.

cape (noun) A **cape** is a long coat that has no sleeves and goes over your body and arms.

fight (verb) If you **fight** someone, you try to hurt them.

hole (noun) A **hole** in something is a part of it that is open.

hug (verb) If you **hug** someone, you put your arms around them and hold them close to you, to make them feel better.

mask (noun) A **mask** is something that you wear over your face or eyes.

ninja (noun) A **ninja** is a person in a film or a book who has special skills like fighting and moving very quietly.

win (verb) If you **win**, you do better than everyone in a game or a competition.

1 Look and order the story

2 Listen and say

Collins

Published by Collins
An imprint of HarperCollins*Publishers*
Westerhill Road
Bishopbriggs
Glasgow
G64 2QT

HarperCollins*Publishers*
1st Floor, Watermarque Building
Ringsend Road
Dublin 4
Ireland

William Collins' dream of knowledge for all began with the publication of his first book in 1819.

A self-educated mill worker, he not only enriched millions of lives, but also founded a flourishing publishing house. Today, staying true to this spirit, Collins books are packed with inspiration, innovation and practical expertise. They place you at the centre of a world of possibility and give you exactly what you need to explore it.

© HarperCollins*Publishers* Limited 2020

10 9 8 7 6 5 4 3 2

ISBN 978-0-00-839755-5

Collins® and COBUILD® are registered trademarks of HarperCollins*Publishers* Limited

www.collins.co.uk/elt

British Library Cataloguing in Publication Data

A catalogue record for this publication is available from the British Library.

Author: Catherine Baker
Illustrator: Jan Smith (Beehive)
Series editor: Rebecca Adlard
Commissioning editor: Zoë Clarke
Publishing manager: Lisa Todd
Product managers: Jennifer Hall and Caroline Green
In-house editor: Alma Puts Keren
Project manager: Emily Hooton
Editor: Matthew Hancock
Proofreaders: Natalie Murray and Michael Lamb
Cover designer: Kevin Robbins
Typesetter: 2Hoots Publishing Services Ltd
Audio produced by id audio, London
Reading guide author: Emma Wilkinson
Production controller: Rachel Weaver
Printed and bound by: GPS Group, Slovenia

Download the audio for this book and a reading guide for parents and teachers at www.collins.co.uk/839755